DOVER·THRIFT·EDITIONS

Sonnets from the Portuguese and Other Poems

ELIZABETH BARRETT BROWNING

DOVER PUBLICATIONS, INC.
New York

DOVER THRIFT EDITIONS
Editor: Stanley Appelbaum

Copyright © 1992 by Dover Publications, Inc.
All rights reserved under Pan American and International Copyright Conventions.

Published in Canada by General Publishing Company, Ltd., 30 Lesmill Road, Don Mills, Toronto, Ontario.
Published in the United Kingdom by Constable and Company, Ltd., 3 The Lanchesters, 162–164 Fulham Palace Road, London W6 9ER.

This Dover edition, first published in 1992, is a new anthology of 20 works (counting the *Sonnets from the Portuguese* as one work) reprinted in their entirety from *The Complete Poetical Works of Elizabeth Barrett Browning: Cambridge Edition*, originally published by the Houghton Mifflin Company, Boston (The Riverside Press, Cambridge), 1900. The Note, table of contents and alphabetical lists were prepared specially for the present edition.

Manufactured in the United States of America
Dover Publications, Inc.
31 East 2nd Street
Mineola, N.Y. 11501

Library of Congress Cataloging-in-Publication Data

Browning, Elizabeth Barrett, 1806–1861.
    Sonnets from the Portuguese, and other poems / Elizabeth Barrett Browning.
       p.   cm. — (Dover thrift editions)
   ISBN 0-486-27052-1
   I. Title. II. Series.
PR4189.A1 1992
821'.8—dc20
                                                                        91-28201
                                                                          CIP

Note

THE ENGLISH POET Elizabeth Barrett (1806–1861) married the poet Robert Browning in 1846; her invalid spinsterhood and the couple's romantic courtship were made familiar to a wide audience by the play *The Barretts of Wimpole Street* and its film versions. Mrs. Browning is best known for her remarkable sequence of 44 love poems *Sonnets from the Portuguese* (they were completely original, but her husband, to whom they were addressed, suggested the whimsical artifice). Many other poems by Mrs. Browning deal with love and woman's psychology, but an important segment of her work is also concerned with religion, art, social problems and political events. The present anthology attempts to be fair to the full scope of her inspiration.

Contents

Dates following titles of individual poems refer to initial magazine publication.

From *The Seraphim and other Poems* (1838)

The Sleep	1
A Sea-Side Walk	3
Consolation	4

From *Poems* (1844)

Grief	4
Cheerfulness Taught by Reason	5
To George Sand: A Desire	6
To George Sand: A Recognition	6
The Cry of the Children (1843)	7
To Flush, My Dog (1843)	12
The Cry of the Human (1842)	16

From *Poems* (1850)

Two Sketches [Henrietta and Arabella Barrett, the poet's sisters] (1847)	20
Hiram Powers' 'Greek Slave'	21
A Woman's Shortcomings (1846)	21
Life and Love	23

Contents

Sonnets from the Portuguese (1850) — 24

From *Poems before Congress* (1860)
    A Curse for a Nation — 42

From *Last Poems* (1862)
    A False Step — 46
    Amy's Cruelty — 47
    A Musical Instrument (1860) — 49
    The Forced Recruit (1860) — 50

Alphabetical List of Titles — 53
Alphabetical List of First Lines — 54

The Sleep

'He giveth His beloved sleep.'
—*Psalm* cxxvii. 2.

I

Of all the thoughts of God that are
Borne inward into souls afar,
Along the Psalmist's music deep,
Now tell me if that any is,
For gift or grace, surpassing this:
'He giveth his belovèd—sleep?'

II

What would we give to our beloved?
The hero's heart to be unmoved,
The poet's star-tuned harp to sweep,
The patriot's voice to teach and rouse,
The monarch's crown to light the brows?
He giveth his belovèd—sleep.

III

What do we give to our beloved?
A little faith all undisproved,
A little dust to overweep,
And bitter memories to make
The whole earth blasted for our sake:
He giveth his belovèd—sleep.

IV

'Sleep soft,' beloved! we sometimes say,
Who have no tune to charm away
Sad dreams that through the eyelids creep:
But never doleful dream again
Shall break the happy slumber when
He giveth his belovèd—sleep.

V

O earth, so full of dreary noises !
O men, with wailing in your voices !
O delvèd gold, the wailers heap !
O strife, O curse, that o'er it fall !
God strikes a silence through you all,
And giveth his belovèd—sleep.

VI

His dews drop mutely on the hill,
His cloud above it saileth still,
Though on its slope men sow and reap:
More softly than the dew is shed,
Or cloud is floated overhead,
He giveth his belovèd—sleep.

VII

Ay, men may wonder while they scan
A living, thinking, feeling man
Confirmed in such a rest to keep;
But angels say, and through the word
I think their happy smile is *heard*—
' He giveth his belovèd—sleep.'

VIII

For me, my heart that erst did go
Most like a tired child at a show,
That sees through tears the mummers leap,
Would now its wearied vision close,
Would childlike on his love repose
Who giveth his belovèd—sleep.

IX

And friends, dear friends, when it shall be
That this low breath is gone from me,
And round my bier ye come to weep,
Let One, most loving of you all,
Say ' Not a tear must o'er her fall !
' He giveth his belovèd sleep.'

A Sea-Side Walk

I

We walked beside the sea
After a day which perished silently
Of its own glory—like the princess weird
Who, combating the Genius, scorched and seared,
Uttered with burning breath, ' Ho ! victory ! '
And sank adown, a heap of ashes pale:
    So runs the Arab tale.

II

The sky above us showed
A universal and unmoving cloud
On which the cliffs permitted us to see
Only the outline of their majesty,
As master-minds when gazed at by the crowd:
And shining with a gloom, the water gray
    Swang in its moon-taught way.

III

Nor moon, nor stars were out;
They did not dare to tread so soon about,
Though trembling, in the footsteps of the sun:
The light was neither night's nor day's, but one
Which, life-like, had a beauty in its doubt,
And silence's impassioned breathings round
    Seemed wandering into sound.

IV

O solemn-beating heart
Of nature ! I have knowledge that thou art
Bound unto man's by cords he cannot sever;
And, what time they are slackened by him ever,
So to attest his own supernal part,
Still runneth thy vibration fast and strong
    The slackened cord along:

V
For though we never spoke
Of the gray water and the shaded rock,
Dark wave and stone unconsciously were fused
Into the plaintive speaking that we used
Of absent friends and memories unforsook;
And, had we seen each other's face, we had
    Seen haply each was sad.

Consolation

All are not taken; there are left behind
Living Belovèds, tender looks to bring
And make the daylight still a happy thing,
And tender voices, to make soft the wind:
But if it were not so—if I could find
No love in all the world for comforting,
Nor any path but hollowly did ring
Where ' dust to dust ' the love from life disjoined,
And if, before those sepulchres unmoving
I stood alone, (as some forsaken lamb
Goes bleating up the moors in weary dearth,)
Crying ' Where are ye, O my loved and loving ? '—
I know a Voice would sound, ' Daughter, I AM.
Can I suffice for HEAVEN and not for earth ? '

Grief

I tell you, hopeless grief is passionless;
That only men incredulous of despair,
Half-taught in anguish, through the midnight air
Beat upward to God's throne in loud access

Of shrieking and reproach. Full desertness,
In souls as countries, lieth silent-bare
Under the blanching, vertical eye-glare
Of the absolute Heavens. Deep-hearted man, express
Grief for thy Dead in silence like to death—
Most like a monumental statue set
In everlasting watch and moveless woe
Till itself crumble to the dust beneath.
Touch it; the marble eyelids are not wet:
If it could weep, it could arise and go.

Cheerfulness Taught by Reason

I think we are too ready with complaint
In this fair world of God's. Had we no hope
Indeed beyond the zenith and the slope
Of yon gray blank of sky, we might grow faint
To muse upon eternity's constraint
Round our aspirant souls; but since the scope
Must widen early, is it well to droop,
For a few days consumed in loss and taint?
O pusillanimous Heart, be comforted
And, like a cheerful traveller, take the road,
Singing beside the hedge. What if the bread
Be bitter in thine inn, and thou unshod
To meet the flints? At least it may be said
'Because the way is *short*, I thank thee, God.'

To George Sand

A DESIRE

Thou large-brained woman and large-hearted man,
Self-called George Sand ! whose soul, amid the lions
Of thy tumultuous senses, moans defiance
And answers roar for roar, as spirits can:
I would some mild miraculous thunder ran
Above the applauded circus, in appliance
Of thine own nobler nature's strength and science,
Drawing two pinions, white as wings of swan,
From thy strong shoulders, to amaze the place
With holier light ! that thou to woman's claim
And man's, mightst join beside the angel's grace
Of a pure genius sanctified from blame,
Till child and maiden pressed to thine embrace
To kiss upon thy lips a stainless fame.

To George Sand

A RECOGNITION

True genius, but true woman ! dost deny
The woman's nature with a manly scorn,
And break away the gauds and armlets worn
By weaker women in captivity ?
Ah, vain denial ! that revolted cry
Is sobbed in by a woman's voice forlorn,—
Thy woman's hair, my sister, all unshorn
Floats back dishevelled strength in agony,
Disproving thy man's name: and while before
The world thou burnest in a poet-fire,
We see thy woman-heart beat evermore

Through the large flame. Beat purer, heart, and higher,
Till God unsex thee on the heavenly shore
Where unincarnate spirits purely aspire !

The Cry of the Children

' Φεῦ, φεῦ, τί προσδέρκεσθέ μ' ὄμμασιν, τέκνα; '
—*Medea*.

I

Do ye hear the children weeping, O my brothers,
    Ere the sorrow comes with years ?
They are leaning their young heads against their mothers,
    And *that* cannot stop their tears.
The young lambs are bleating in the meadows,
    The young birds are chirping in the nest,
The young fawns are playing with the shadows,
    The young flowers are blowing toward the west—
But the young, young children, O my brothers,
    They are weeping bitterly !
They are weeping in the playtime of the others,
    In the country of the free.

II

Do you question the young children in the sorrow
    Why their tears are falling so ?
The old man may weep for his to-morrow
    Which is lost in Long Ago;
The old tree is leafless in the forest,
    The old year is ending in the frost,
The old wound, if stricken, is the sorest,
    The old hope is hardest to be lost:
But the young, young children, O my brothers,
    Do you ask them why they stand
Weeping sore before the bosoms of their mothers,
    In our happy Fatherland ?

III

They look up with their pale and sunken faces,
  And their looks are sad to see,
For the man's hoary anguish draws and presses
  Down the cheeks of infancy;
' Your old earth,' they say, ' is very dreary,
  Our young feet,' they say, ' are very weak;
Few paces have we taken, yet are weary—
  Our grave-rest is very far to seek:
Ask the aged why they weep, and not the children,
  For the outside earth is cold,
And we young ones stand without, in our bewildering,
  And the graves are for the old.

IV

' True,' say the children, ' it may happen
  That we die before our time:
Little Alice died last year, her grave is shapen
  Like a snowball, in the rime.
We looked into the pit prepared to take her:
  Was no room for any work in the close clay !
From the sleep wherein she lieth none will wake her,
  Crying, " Get up, little Alice ! it is day."
If you listen by that grave, in sun and shower,
  With your ear down, little Alice never cries;
Could we see her face, be sure we should not know her,
  For the smile has time for growing in her eyes:
And merry go her moments, lulled and stilled in
  The shroud by the kirk-chime.
It is good when it happens,' say the children,
  ' That we die before our time.'

V

Alas, alas, the children ! they are seeking
  Death in life, as best to have:
They are binding up their hearts away from breaking,
  With a cerement from the grave.
Go out, children, from the mine and from the city,
  Sing out, children, as the little thrushes do;

Pluck your handfuls of the meadow-cowslips pretty.
    Laugh aloud, to feel your fingers let them through !
But they answer, ' Are your cowslips of the meadows
    Like our weeds anear the mine ?
Leave us quiet in the dark of the coal-shadows,
    From your pleasures fair and fine !

VI

' For oh,' say the children, ' we are weary,
    And we cannot run or leap;
If we cared for any meadows, it were merely
    To drop down in them and sleep.
Our knees tremble sorely in the stooping,
    We fall upon our faces, trying to go;
And, underneath our heavy eyelids drooping
    The reddest flower would look as pale as snow.
For, all day, we drag our burden tiring
    Through the coal-dark, underground;
Or, all day, we drive the wheels of iron
    In the factories, round and round.

VII

' For all day the wheels are droning, turning;
    Their wind comes in our faces,
Till our hearts turn, our heads with pulses burning,
    And the walls turn in their places:
Turns the sky in the high window, blank and reeling,
    Turns the long light that drops adown the wall,
Turn the black flies that crawl along the ceiling:
    All are turning, all the day, and we with all.
And all day the iron wheels are droning,
    And sometimes we could pray,
" O ye wheels " (breaking out in a mad moaning),
    " Stop ! be silent for to-day ! " '

VIII

Ay, be silent ! Let them hear each other breathing
    For a moment, mouth to mouth !
Let them touch each other's hands, in a fresh wreathing
    Of their tender human youth !

Let them feel that this cold metallic motion
   Is not all the life God fashions or reveals:
Let them prove their living souls against the notion
   That they live in you, or under you, O wheels !
Still, all day, the iron wheels go onward,
   Grinding life down from its mark;
And the children's souls, which God is calling sunward,
   Spin on blindly in the dark.

IX

Now tell the poor young children, O my brothers,
   To look up to Him and pray;
So the blessèd One who blesseth all the others,
   Will bless them another day.
They answer, ' Who is God that He should hear us,
   While the rushing of the iron wheels is stirred ?
When we sob aloud, the human creatures near us
   Pass by, hearing not, or answer not a word.
And *we* hear not (for the wheels in their resounding)
   Strangers speaking at the door:
Is it likely God, with angels singing round Him,
   Hears our weeping any more ?

X

' Two words, indeed, of praying we remember,
   And at midnight's hour of harm,
" Our Father," looking upward in the chamber,
   We say softly for a charm.
We know no other words except " Our Father,"
   And we think that, in some pause of angels' song,
God may pluck them with the silence sweet to gather,
   And hold both within his right hand which is strong.
" Our Father ! " If He heard us, He would surely
   (For they call Him good and mild)
Answer, smiling down the steep world very purely,
   " Come and rest with me, my child."

XI

' But, no ! ' say the children, weeping faster,
    ' He is speechless as a stone:
And they tell us, of His image is the master
    Who commands us to work on.
Go to ! ' say the children,—' up in Heaven,
    Dark, wheel-like, turning clouds are all we find.
Do not mock us; grief has made us unbelieving:
    We look up for God, but tears have made us blind.'
Do you hear the children weeping and disproving,
    O my brothers, what ye preach ?
For God's possible is taught by his world's loving,
    And the children doubt of each.

XII

And well may the children weep before you !
    They are weary ere they run;
They have never seen the sunshine, nor the glory
    Which is brighter than the sun.
They know the grief of man, without its wisdom;
    They sink in man's despair, without its calm;
Are slaves, without the liberty in Christdom,
    Are martyrs, by the pang without the palm:
Are worn as if with age, yet unretrievingly
    The harvest of its memories cannot reap,—
Are orphans of the earthly love and heavenly.
    Let them weep ! let them weep !

XIII

They look up with their pale and sunken faces,
    And their look is dread to see,
For they mind you of their angels in high places,
    With eyes turned on Deity.
' How long,' they say, ' how long, O cruel nation,
    Will you stand, to move the world, on a child's heart,—
Stifle down with a mailèd heel its palpitation,
    And tread onward to your throne amid the mart ?
Our blood splashes upward, O gold-heaper,

And your purple shows your path !
But the child's sob in the silence curses deeper
Than the strong man in his wrath.'

To Flush, My Dog

I

Loving friend, the gift of one
Who her own true faith has run
   Through thy lower nature,
Be my benediction said
With my hand upon thy head,
   Gentle fellow-creature !

II

Like a lady's ringlets brown,
Flow thy silken ears adown
   Either side demurely
Of thy silver-suited breast
Shining out from all the rest
   Of thy body purely.

III

Darkly brown thy body is,
Till the sunshine striking this
   Alchemize its dulness,
When the sleek curls manifold
Flash all over into gold
   With a burnished fulness.

IV

Underneath my stroking hand,
Startled eyes of hazel bland
   Kindling, growing larger,
Up thou leapest with a spring,
Full of prank and curveting,
   Leaping like a charger.

V

Leap ! thy broad tail waves a light,
Leap ! thy slender feet are bright,
   Canopied in fringes;
Leap ! those tasselled ears of thine
Flicker strangely, fair and fine
   Down their golden inches.

VI

Yet, my pretty, sportive friend,
Little is 't to such an end
   That I praise thy rareness;
Other dogs may be thy peers
Haply in these drooping ears
   And this glossy fairness.

VII

But of *thee* it shall be said,
This dog watched beside a bed
   Day and night unweary,
Watched within a curtained room
Where no sunbeam brake the gloom
   Round the sick and dreary.

VIII

Roses, gathered for a vase,
In that chamber died apace,
   Beam and breeze resigning;
This dog only, waited on,
Knowing that when light is gone
   Love remains for shining.

IX

Other dogs in thymy dew
Tracked the hares and followed through
   Sunny moor or meadow;
This dog only, crept and crept
Next a languid cheek that slept,
   Sharing in the shadow.

X

Other dogs of loyal cheer
Bounded at the whistle clear,
  Up the woodside hieing;
This dog only, watched in reach
Of a faintly uttered speech
  Or a louder sighing.

XI

And if one or two quick tears
Dropped upon his glossy ears
  Or a sigh came double,
Up he sprang in eager haste,
Fawning, fondling, breathing fast,
  In a tender trouble.

XII

And this dog was satisfied
If a pale thin hand would glide
  Down his dewlaps sloping,—
Which he pushed his nose within,
After,—platforming his chin
  On the palm left open.

XIII

This dog, if a friendly voice
Call him now to blither choice
  Than such chamber-keeping,
' Come out ! ' praying from the door,—
Presseth backward as before,
  Up against me leaping.

XIV

Therefore to this dog will I,
Tenderly not scornfully,
  Render praise and favor:
With my hand upon his head,
Is my benediction said
  Therefore and for ever.

XV

And because he loves me so,
Better than his kind will do
   Often man or woman,
Give I back more love again
Than dogs often take of men,
   Leaning from my Human.

XVI

Blessings on thee, dog of mine,
Pretty collars make thee fine,
   Sugared milk make fat thee!
Pleasures wag on in thy tail,
Hands of gentle motion fail
   Nevermore, to pat thee!

XVII

Downy pillow take thy head,
Silken coverlid bestead,
   Sunshine help thy sleeping!
No fly's buzzing wake thee up,
No man break thy purple cup
   Set for drinking deep in.

XVIII

Whiskered cats arointed flee,
Sturdy stoppers keep from thee
   Cologne distillations;
Nuts lie in thy path for stones,
And thy feast-day macaroons
   Turn to daily rations!

XIX

Mock I thee, in wishing weal?—
Tears are in my eyes to feel
   Thou art made so straitly,
Blessing needs must straiten too,—
Little canst thou joy or do,
   Thou who lovest *greatly*.

XX

 Yet be blessèd to the height
 Of all good and all delight
  Pervious to thy nature;
 Only *loved* beyond that line,
 With a love that answers thine,
  Loving fellow-creature !

The Cry of the Human

I

' There is no God ' the foolish saith,
 But none ' There is no sorrow,'
And nature oft the cry of faith
 In bitter need will borrow:
Eyes, which the preacher could not school,
 By wayside graves are raisèd,
And lips say ' God be pitiful,'
 Who ne'er said ' God be praisèd.'
     Be pitiful, O God !

II

The tempest stretches from the steep
 The shadow of its coming,
The beasts grow tame and near us creep,
 As help were in the human;
Yet, while the cloud-wheels roll and grind,
 We spirits tremble under—
The hills have echoes, but we find
 No answer for the thunder.
     Be pitiful, O God !

III

The battle hurtles on the plains,
 Earth feels new scythes upon her;
We reap our brothers for the wains,

And call the harvest—honor:
Draw face to face, front line to line,
    One image all inherit,—
Then kill, curse on, by that same sign,
    Clay—clay, and spirit—spirit.
                Be pitiful, O God !

IV

The plague runs festering through the town,
    And never a bell is tolling,
And corpses, jostled 'neath the moon,
    Nod to the dead-cart's rolling:
The young child calleth for the cup,
    The strong man brings it weeping,
The mother from her babe looks up,
    And shrieks away its sleeping.
                Be pitiful, O God !

V

The plague of gold strikes far and near,
    And deep and strong it enters;
This purple chimar which we wear
    Makes madder than the centaur's:
Our thoughts grow blank, our words grow strange,
    We cheer the pale gold-diggers,
Each soul is worth so much on 'Change,
    And marked, like sheep, with figures.
                Be pitiful, O God !

VI

The curse of gold upon the land
    The lack of bread enforces;
The rail-cars snort from strand to strand,
    Like more of Death's White Horses:
The rich preach ' rights ' and ' future days,'
    And hear no angel scoffing,
The poor die mute, with starving gaze
    On corn-ships in the offing.
                Be pitiful, O God !

VII

We meet together at the feast,
    To private mirth betake us;
We stare down in the winecup, lest
    Some vacant chair should shake us:
We name delight, and pledge it round—
    ' It shall be ours to-morrow ! '
God's seraphs, do your voices sound
    As sad, in naming sorrow ?
                Be pitiful, O God !

VIII

We sit together, with the skies,
    The steadfast skies, above us,
We look into each other's eyes,
    ' And how long will you love us ? '
The eyes grow dim with prophecy,
    The voices, low and breathless,—
' Till death us part ! '—O words, to be
    Our *best*, for love the deathless !
                Be pitiful, O God !

IX

We tremble by the harmless bed
    Of one loved and departed:
Our tears drop on the lips that said
    Last night ' Be stronger-hearted ! '
O God—to clasp those fingers close,
    And yet to feel so lonely !
To see a light upon such brows,
    Which is the daylight only !
                Be pitiful, O God !

X

The happy children come to us
    And look up in our faces;
They ask us ' Was it thus, and thus,
    When we were in their places ? '
We cannot speak;—we see anew
    The hills we used to live in,

And feel our mother's smile press through
    The kisses she is giving.
                Be pitiful, O God !

XI

We pray together at the kirk
    For mercy, mercy solely:
Hands weary with the evil work,
    We lift them to the Holy.
The corpse is calm below our knee,
    Its spirit, bright before Thee:
Between them, worse than either, we—
    Without the rest or glory.
                Be pitiful, O God !

XII

We leave the communing of men,
    The murmur of the passions,
And live alone, to live again
    With endless generations:
Are we so brave ? The sea and sky
    In silence lift their mirrors,
And, glassed therein, our spirits high
    Recoil from their own terrors.
                Be pitiful, O God !

XIII

We sit on hills our childhood wist,
    Woods, hamlets, streams, beholding
The sun strikes through the farthest mist
    The city's spire to golden:
The city's golden spire it was,
    When hope and health were strongest,
But now it is the churchyard grass
    We look upon the longest.
                Be pitiful, O God !

XIV

And soon all vision waxeth dull;
    Men whisper ' He is dying;'
We cry no more ' Be pitiful ! '

  We have no strength for crying:
 No strength, no need. Then, soul of mine,
  Look up and triumph rather !
 Lo, in the depth of God's Divine,
  The Son adjures the Father,
      BE PITIFUL, O GOD !

Two Sketches

I
H. B.

The shadow of her face upon the wall
May take your memory to the perfect Greek,
But when you front her, you would call the cheek
Too full, sir, for your models, if withal
That bloom it wears could leave you critical,
And that smile reaching toward the rosy streak;
For one who smiles so has no need to speak
To lead your thoughts along, as steed to stall.
A smile that turns the sunny side o' the heart
On all the world, as if herself did win
By what she lavished on an open mart !
Let no man call the liberal sweetness, sin,—
For friends may whisper as they stand apart,
' Methinks there 's still some warmer place within.'

II
A. B.

Her azure eyes, dark lashes hold in fee;
Her fair superfluous ringlets without check
Drop after one another down her neck,
As many to each cheek as you might see
Green leaves to a wild rose; this sign outwardly,
And a like woman-covering seems to deck
Her inner nature, for she will not fleck

World's sunshine with a finger. Sympathy
Must call her in Love's name ! and then, I know,
She rises up, and brightens as she should,
And lights her smile for comfort, and is slow
In nothing of high-hearted fortitude.
To smell this flower, come near it ! such can grow
In that sole garden where Christ's brow dropped blood.

Hiram Powers' ' Greek Slave '

They say Ideal beauty cannot enter
The house of anguish. On the threshold stands
An alien Image with enshackled hands,
Called the Greek Slave ! as if the artist meant her
(That passionless perfection which he lent her,
Shadowed not darkened where the sill expands)
To so confront man's crimes in different lands
With man's ideal sense. Pierce to the centre,
Art's fiery finger, and break up ere long
The serfdom of this world. Appeal, fair stone,
From God's pure heights of beauty against man's wrong !
Catch up in thy divine face, not alone
East griefs but west, and strike and shame the strong,
By thunders of white silence, overthrown.

A Woman's Shortcomings

I

She has laughed as softly as if she sighed,
   She has counted six, and over,
Of a purse well filled and a heart well tried—

Oh, each a worthy lover !
They ' give her time;' for her soul must slip
   Where the world has set the grooving;
She will lie to none with her fair red lip:
   But love seeks truer loving.

II

She trembles her fan in a sweetness dumb,
   As her thoughts were beyond recalling,
With a glance for *one*, and a glance for *some*,
   From her eyelids rising and falling;
Speaks common words with a blushful air,
   Hears bold words, unreproving;
But her silence says—what she never will swear—
   And love seeks better loving.

III

Go, lady, lean to the night-guitar
   And drop a smile to the bringer;
Then smile as sweetly, when he is far,
   At the voice of an in-door singer.
Bask tenderly beneath tender eyes;
   Glance lightly, on their removing;
And join new vows to old perjuries—
   But dare not call it loving.

IV

Unless you can think, when the song is done,
   No other is soft in the rhythm;
Unless you can feel, when left by One,
   That all men else go with him;
Unless you can know, when unpraised by his breath,
   That your beauty itself wants proving;
Unless you can swear ' For life, for death ! '—
   Oh, fear to call it loving !

V

Unless you can muse in a crowd all day
  On the absent face that fixed you;
Unless you can love, as the angels may,
  With the breadth of heaven betwixt you;
Unless you can dream that his faith is fast,
  Through behoving and unbehoving;
Unless you can *die* when the dream is past—
  Oh, never call it loving!

Life and Love

I

Fast this Life of mine was dying,
  Blind already and calm as death,
Snowflakes on her bosom lying
  Scarcely heaving with her breath.

II

Love came by, and having known her
  In a dream of fabled lands,
Gently stooped, and laid upon her
  Mystic chrism of holy hands;

III

Drew his smile across her folded
  Eyelids, as the swallow dips;
Breathed as finely as the cold did
  Through the locking of her lips.

IV

So, when Life looked upward, being
  Warmed and breathed on from above,
What sight could she have for seeing,
  Evermore . . . but only LOVE?

Sonnets from the Portuguese

I

I thought once how Theocritus had sung
Of the sweet years, the dear and wished-for years,
Who each one in a gracious hand appears
To bear a gift for mortals, old or young:
And, as I mused it in his antique tongue,
I saw, in gradual vision through my tears,
The sweet, sad years, the melancholy years,
Those of my own life, who by turns had flung
A shadow across me. Straightway I was 'ware,
So weeping, how a mystic Shape did move
Behind me, and drew me backward by the hair:
And a voice said in mastery, while I strove,—
' Guess now who holds thee ? '—' Death,' I said. But,
    there,
The silver answer rang,—' Not Death, but Love.'

II

But only three in all God's universe
Have heard this word thou hast said,—Himself, beside
Thee speaking, and me listening ! and replied
One of us . . . *that* was God, . . . and laid the curse
So darkly on my eyelids, as to amerce
My sight from seeing thee,—that if I had died,
The deathweights, placed there, would have signified
Less absolute exclusion. ' Nay ' is worse
From God than from all others, O my friend !
Men could not part us with their worldly jars,
Nor the seas change us, nor the tempests bend;
Our hands would touch for all the mountain-bars:
And, heaven being rolled between us at the end,
We should but vow the faster for the stars.

III

Unlike are we, unlike, O princely Heart !
Unlike our uses and our destinies.

Our ministering two angels look surprise
On one another, as they strike athwart
Their wings in passing. Thou, bethink thee, art
A guest for queens to social pageantries,
With gages from a hundred brighter eyes
Than tears even can make mine, to play thy part
Of chief musician. What hast *thou* to do
With looking from the lattice-lights at me,
A poor, tired, wandering singer, singing through
The dark, and leaning up a cypress tree?
The chrism is on thine head,—on mine, the dew,—
And Death must dig the level where these agree.

IV

Thou hast thy calling to some palace-floor,
Most gracious singer of high poems! where
The dancers will break footing, from the care
Of watching up thy pregnant lips for more.
And dost thou lift this house's latch too poor
For hand of thine? and canst thou think and bear
To let thy music drop here unaware
In folds of golden fulness at my door?
Look up and see the casement broken in,
The bats and owlets builders in the roof!
My cricket chirps against thy mandolin.
Hush, call no echo up in further proof
Of desolation! there's a voice within
That weeps . . . as thou must sing . . . alone, aloof.

V

I lift my heavy heart up solemnly,
As once Electra her sepulchral urn,
And, looking in thine eyes, I overturn
The ashes at thy feet. Behold and see
What a great heap of grief lay hid in me,
And how the red wild sparkles dimly burn
Through the ashen grayness. If thy foot in scorn
Could tread them out to darkness utterly,

It might be well perhaps. But if instead
Thou wait beside me for the wind to blow
The gray dust up, . . . those laurels on thine head,
O my Belovèd, will not shield thee so,
That none of all the fires shall scorch and shred
The hair beneath. Stand farther off then ! go.

VI

Go from me. Yet I feel that I shall stand
Henceforward in thy shadow. Nevermore
Alone upon the threshold of my door
Of individual life, I shall command
The uses of my soul, nor lift my hand
Serenely in the sunshine as before,
Without the sense of that which I forbore—
Thy touch upon the palm. The widest land
Doom takes to part us, leaves thy heart in mine
With pulses that beat double. What I do
And what I dream include thee, as the wine
Must taste of its own grapes. And when I sue
God for myself, He hears that name of thine,
And sees within my eyes the tears of two.

VII

The face of all the world is changed, I think,
Since first I heard the footsteps of thy soul
Move still, oh, still, beside me, as they stole
Betwixt me and the dreadful outer brink
Of obvious death, where I, who thought to sink,
Was caught up into love, and taught the whole
Of life in a new rhythm. The cup of dole
God gave for baptism, I am fain to drink,
And praise its sweetness, Sweet, with thee anear.
The names of country, heaven, are changed away
For where thou art or shalt be, there or here;
And this . . . this lute and song . . . loved yesterday,
(The singing angels know) are only dear
Because thy name moves right in what they say.

VIII

What can I give thee back, O liberal
And princely giver, who hast brought the gold
And purple of thine heart, unstained, untold,
And laid them on the outside of the wall
For such as I to take or leave withal,
In unexpected largesse? am I cold,
Ungrateful, that for these most manifold
High gifts, I render nothing back at all?
Not so; not cold,—but very poor instead.
Ask God who knows. For frequent tears have run
The colors from my life, and left so dead
And pale a stuff, it were not fitly done
To give the same as pillow to thy head.
Go farther! let it serve to trample on.

IX

Can it be right to give what I can give?
To let thee sit beneath the fall of tears
As salt as mine, and hear the sighing years
Re-sighing on my lips renunciative
Through those infrequent smiles which fail to live
For all thy adjurations? O my fears,
That this can scarce be right! We are not peers,
So to be lovers; and I own, and grieve,
That givers of such gifts as mine are, must
Be counted with the ungenerous. Out, alas!
I will not soil thy purple with my dust,
Nor breathe my poison on thy Venice-glass,
Nor give thee any love—which were unjust.
Beloved, I only love thee! let it pass.

X

Yet, love, mere love, is beautiful indeed
And worthy of acceptation. Fire is bright,
Let temple burn, or flax; an equal light
Leaps in the flame from cedar-plank or weed:
And love is fire. And when I say at need

I love thee . . . mark ! . . . *I love thee*—in thy sight
I stand transfigured, glorified aright,
With conscience of the new rays that proceed
Out of my face toward thine. There's nothing low
In love, when love the lowest: meanest creatures
Who love God, God accepts while loving so.
And what I *feel*, across the inferior features
Of what I *am*, doth flash itself, and show
How that great work of Love enhances Nature's.

XI

And therefore if to love can be desert,
I am not all unworthy. Cheeks as pale
As these you see, and trembling knees that fail
To bear the burden of a heavy heart,—
This weary minstrel-life that once was girt
To climb Aornus, and can scarce avail
To pipe now 'gainst the valley nightingale
A melancholy music,—why advert
To these things ? O Belovèd, it is plain
I am not of thy worth nor for thy place !
And yet, because I love thee, I obtain
From that same love this vindicating grace,
To live on still in love, and yet in vain,—
To bless thee, yet renounce thee to thy face.

XII

Indeed this very love which is my boast,
And which, when rising up from breast to brow,
Doth crown me with a ruby large enow
To draw men's eyes and prove the inner cost,—
This love even, all my worth, to the uttermost,
I should not love withal, unless that thou
Hadst set me an example, shown me how,
When first thine earnest eyes with mine were crossed,
And love called love. And thus, I cannot speak
Of love even, as a good thing of my own:
Thy soul hath snatched up mine all faint and weak,

And placed it by thee on a golden throne,—
And that I love (O soul, we must be meek !)
Is by thee only, whom I love alone.

XIII

And wilt thou have me fashion into speech
The love I bear thee, finding words enough,
And hold the torch out, while the winds are rough,
Between our faces, to cast light on each ?—
I drop it at thy feet. I cannot teach
My hand to hold my spirit so far off
From myself—me—that I should bring thee proof
In words, of love hid in me out of reach.
Nay, let the silence of my womanhood
Commend my woman-love to thy belief,—
Seeing that I stand unwon, however wooed,
And rend the garment of my life, in brief,
By a most dauntless, voiceless fortitude,
Lest one touch of this heart convey its grief.

XIV

If thou must love me, let it be for nought
Except for love's sake only. Do not say
' I love her for her smile—her look—her way
Of speaking gently,—for a trick of thought
That falls in well with mine, and certes brought
A sense of pleasant ease on such a day '—
For these things in themselves, Belovèd, may
Be changed, or change for thee,—and love, so wrought,
May be unwrought so. Neither love me for
Thine own dear pity's wiping my cheeks dry,—
A creature might forget to weep, who bore
Thy comfort long, and lose thy love thereby !
But love me for love's sake, that evermore
Thou mayst love on, through love's eternity.

XV

Accuse me not, beseech thee, that I wear
Too calm and sad a face in front of thine;
For we two look two ways, and cannot shine
With the same sunlight on our brow and hair.
On me thou lookest with no doubting care,
As on a bee shut in a crystalline;
Since sorrow hath shut me safe in love's divine,
And to spread wing and fly in the outer air
Were most impossible failure, if I strove
To fail so. But I look on thee—on thee—
Beholding, besides love, the end of love,
Hearing oblivion beyond memory;
As one who sits and gazes from above,
Over the rivers to the bitter sea.

XVI

And yet, because thou overcomest so,
Because thou art more noble and like a king,
Thou canst prevail against my fears and fling
Thy purple round me, till my heart shall grow
Too close against thine heart henceforth to know
How it shook when alone. Why, conquering
May prove as lordly and complete a thing
In lifting upward, as in crushing low !
And as a vanquished soldier yields his sword
To one who lifts him from the bloody earth,
Even so, Belovèd, I at last record,
Here ends my strife. If *thou* invite me forth,
I rise above abasement at the word.
Make thy love larger to enlarge my worth.

XVII

My poet, thou canst touch on all the notes
God set between his After and Before,
And strike up and strike off the general roar
Of the rushing worlds a melody that floats
In a serene air purely. Antidotes

Of medicated music, answering for
Mankind's forlornest uses, thou canst pour
From thence into their ears. God's will devotes
Thine to such ends, and mine to wait on thine.
How, Dearest, wilt thou have me for most use?
A hope, to sing by gladly? or a fine
Sad memory, with thy songs to interfuse?
A shade, in which to sing—of palm or pine?
A grave, on which to rest from singing? Choose.

XVIII

I never gave a lock of hair away
To a man, Dearest, except this to thee,
Which now upon my fingers thoughtfully,
I ring out to the full brown length and say
'Take it.' My day of youth went yesterday;
My hair no longer bounds to my foot's glee,
Nor plant I it from rose or myrtle-tree,
As girls do, any more: it only may
Now shade on two pale cheeks the mark of tears,
Taught drooping from the head that hangs aside
Through sorrow's trick. I thought the funeral-shears
Would take this first, but Love is justified,—
Take it thou,—finding pure, from all those years,
The kiss my mother left here when she died.

XIX

The soul's Rialto hath its merchandise;
I barter curl for curl upon that mart,
And from my poet's forehead to my heart
Receive this lock which outweighs argosies,—
As purply black, as erst to Pindar's eyes
The dim purpureal tresses gloomed athwart
The nine white Muse-brows. For this counterpart, . . .
The bay-crown's shade, Belovèd, I surmise,
Still lingers on thy curl, it is so black!
Thus, with a fillet of smooth-kissing breath,
I tie the shadows safe from gliding back,

And lay the gift where nothing hindereth;
Here on my heart, as on thy brow, to lack
No natural heat till mine grows cold in death.

XX

Belovèd, my Belovèd, when I think
That thou wast in the world a year ago,
What time I sat alone here in the snow
And saw no footprint, heard the silence sink
No moment at thy voice, but, link by link,
Went counting all my chains as if that so
They never could fall off at any blow
Struck by thy possible hand,—why, thus I drink
Of life's great cup of wonder ! Wonderful,
Never to feel thee thrill the day or night
With personal act or speech,—nor ever cull
Some prescience of thee with the blossoms white
Thou sawest growing ! Atheists are as dull,
Who cannot guess God's presence out of sight.

XXI

Say over again, and yet once over again,
That thou dost love me. Though the word repeated
Should seem ' a cuckoo-song,' as thou dost treat it,
Remember, never to the hill or plain,
Valley and wood, without her cuckoo-strain
Comes the fresh Spring in all her green completed.
Belovèd, I, amid the darkness greeted
By a doubtful spirit-voice, in that doubt's pain
Cry, ' Speak once more—thou lovest ! ' Who can fear
Too many stars, though each in heaven shall roll,
Too many flowers, though each shall crown the year ?
Say thou dost love me, love me, love me—toll
The silver iterance !—only minding, Dear,
To love me also in silence with thy soul.

XXII

When our two souls stand up erect and strong,
Face to face, silent, drawing nigh and nigher,
Until the lengthening wings break into fire

At either curvèd point,—what bitter wrong
Can the earth do to us, that we should not long
Be here contented ? Think. In mounting higher,
The angels would press on us and aspire
To drop some golden orb of perfect song
Into our deep, dear silence. Let us stay
Rather on earth, Belovèd,—where the unfit
Contrarious moods of men recoil away
And isolate pure spirits, and permit
A place to stand and love in for a day,
With darkness and the death-hour rounding it.

XXIII

Is it indeed so ? If I lay here dead,
Wouldst thou miss any life in losing mine ?
And would the sun for thee more coldly shine
Because of grave-damps falling round my head ?
I marvelled, my Belovèd, when I read
Thy thought so in the letter. I am thine—
But . . . *so* much to thee ? Can I pour thy wine
While my hands tremble ? Then my soul, instead
Of dreams of death, resumes life's lower range.
Then, love me, Love ! look on me—breathe on me !
As brighter ladies do not count it strange,
For love, to give up acres and degree,
I yield the grave for thy sake, and exchange
My near sweet view of Heaven, for earth with thee !

XXIV

Let the world's sharpness, like a clasping knife,
Shut in upon itself and do no harm
In this close hand of Love, now soft and warm,
And let us hear no sound of human strife
After the click of the shutting. Life to life—
I lean upon thee, Dear, without alarm,
And feel as safe as guarded by a charm
Against the stab of worldlings, who if rife
Are weak to injure. Very whitely still
The lilies of our lives may reassure

Their blossoms from their roots, accessible
Alone to heavenly dews that drop not fewer,
Growing straight, out of man's reach, on the hill.
God only, who made us rich, can make us poor.

XXV

A heavy heart, Belovèd, have I borne
From year to year until I saw thy face,
And sorrow after sorrow took the place
Of all those natural joys as lightly worn
As the stringed pearls, each lifted in its turn
By a beating heart at dance-time. Hopes apace
Were changed to long despairs, till God's own grace
Could scarcely lift above the world forlorn
My heavy heart. Then *thou* didst bid me bring
And let it drop adown thy calmly great
Deep being ! Fast it sinketh, as a thing
Which its own nature doth precipitate,
While thine doth close above it, mediating
Betwixt the stars and the unaccomplished fate.

XXVI

I lived with visions for my company
Instead of men and women, years ago,
And found them gentle mates, nor thought to know
A sweeter music than they played to me.
But soon their trailing purple was not free
Of this world's dust, their lutes did silent grow,
And I myself grew faint and blind below
Their vanishing eyes. Then THOU didst come—to be,
Belovèd, what they seemed. Their shining fronts,
Their songs, their splendors (better, yet the same,
As river-water hallowed into fonts),
Met in thee, and from out thee overcame
My soul with satisfaction of all wants:
Because God's gifts put man's best dreams to shame.

XXVII

My own Belovèd, who hast lifted me
From this drear flat of earth where I was thrown,
And, in betwixt the languid ringlets, blown
A life-breath, till the forehead hopefully
Shines out again, as all the angels see,
Before thy saving kiss! My own, my own,
Who camest to me when the world was gone,
And I who looked for only God, found *thee*!
I find thee; I am safe, and strong, and glad.
As one who stands in dewless asphodel
Looks backward on the tedious time he had
In the upper life,—so I, with bosom-swell,
Make witness, here, between the good and bad,
That Love, as strong as Death, retrieves as well.

XXVIII

My letters! all dead paper, mute and white!
And yet they seem alive and quivering
Against my tremulous hands which loose the string
And let them drop down on my knee to-night.
This said,—he wished to have me in his sight
Once, as a friend: this fixed a day in spring
To come and touch my hand . . . a simple thing,
Yet I wept for it!—this, . . . the paper's light . . .
Said, *Dear, I love thee*; and I sank and quailed
As if God's future thundered on my past.
This said, *I am thine*—and so its ink has paled
With lying at my heart that beat too fast.
And this . . . O Love, thy words have ill availed
If, what this said, I dared repeat at last!

XXIX

I think of thee!—my thoughts do twine and bud
About thee, as wild vines, about a tree,
Put out broad leaves, and soon there's nought to see
Except the straggling green which hides the wood.

Yet, O my palm-tree, be it understood
I will not have my thoughts instead of thee
Who art dearer, better ! Rather, instantly
Renew thy presence; as a strong tree should,
Rustle thy boughs and set thy trunk all bare,
And let these bands of greenery which insphere thee
Drop heavily down,—burst, shattered, everywhere !
Because, in this deep joy to see and hear thee
And breathe within thy shadow a new air,
I do not think of thee—I am too near thee.

XXX

I see thine image through my tears to-night,
And yet to-day I saw thee smiling. How
Refer the cause ?—Belovèd, is it thou
Or I, who makes me sad ? The acolyte
Amid the chanted joy and thankful rite
May so fall flat, with pale insensate brow,
On the altar-stair. I hear thy voice and vow,
Perplexed, uncertain, since thou art out of sight,
As he, in his swooning ears, the choir's Amen.
Belovèd, dost thou love ? or did I see all
The glory as I dreamed, and fainted when
Too vehement light dilated my ideal,
For my soul's eyes ? Will that light come again,
As now these tears come—falling hot and real ?

XXXI

Thou comest ! all is said without a word.
I sit beneath thy looks, as children do
In the noon-sun, with souls that tremble through
Their happy eyelids from an unaverred
Yet prodigal inward joy. Behold, I erred
In that last doubt ! and yet I cannot rue
The sin most, but the occasion—that we two
Should for a moment stand unministered
By a mutual presence. Ah, keep near and close,
Thou dovelike help ! and, when my fears would rise,
With thy broad heart serenely interpose:

Brood down with thy divine sufficiencies
These thoughts which tremble when bereft of those,
Like callow birds left desert to the skies.

XXXII

The first time that the sun rose on thine oath
To love me, I looked forward to the moon
To slacken all those bonds which seemed too soon
And quickly tied to make a lasting troth.
Quick-loving hearts, I thought, may quickly loathe;
And, looking on myself, I seemed not one
For such man's love !—more like an out-of-tune
Worn viol, a good singer would be wroth
To spoil his song with, and which, snatched in haste,
Is laid down at the first ill-sounding note.
I did not wrong myself so, but I placed
A wrong on *thee*. For perfect strains may float
'Neath master-hands, from instruments defaced,—
And great souls, at one stroke, may do and doat.

XXXIII

Yes, call me by my pet-name ! let me hear
The name I used to run at, when a child,
From innocent play, and leave the cowslips piled,
To glance up in some face that proved me dear
With the look of its eyes. I miss the clear
Fond voices which, being drawn and reconciled
Into the music of Heaven's undefiled,
Call me no longer. Silence on the bier,
While I call God—call God !—So let thy mouth
Be heir to those who are now exanimate.
Gather the north flowers to complete the south,
And catch the early love up in the late.
Yes, call me by that name,—and I, in truth,
With the same heart, will answer and not wait.

XXXIV

With the same heart, I said, I'll answer thee
As those, when thou shalt call me by my name—
Lo, the vain promise ! is the same, the same,

Perplexed and ruffled by life's strategy?
When called before, I told how hastily
I dropped my flowers or brake off from a game,
To run and answer with the smile that came
At play last moment, and went on with me
Through my obedience. When I answer now,
I drop a grave thought, break from solitude;
Yet still my heart goes to thee—ponder how—
Not as to a single good, but all my good!
Lay thy hand on it, best one, and allow
That no child's foot could run fast as this blood.

xxxv

If I leave all for thee, wilt thou exchange
And be all to me? Shall I never miss
Home-talk and blessing and the common kiss
That comes to each in turn, nor count it strange,
When I look up, to drop on a new range
Of walls and floors, another home than this?
Nay, wilt thou fill that place by me which is
Filled by dead eyes too tender to know change?
That's hardest. If to conquer love, has tried,
To conquer grief, tries more, as all things prove;
For grief indeed is love and grief beside.
Alas, I have grieved so I am hard to love.
Yet love me—wilt thou? Open thine heart wide,
And fold within the wet wings of thy dove.

xxxvi

When we met first and loved, I did not build
Upon the event with marble. Could it mean
To last, a love set pendulous between
Sorrow and sorrow? Nay, I rather thrilled,
Distrusting every light that seemed to gild
The onward path, and feared to overlean
A finger even. And, though I have grown serene
And strong since then, I think that God has willed
A still renewable fear . . . O love, O troth . . .
Lest these enclaspèd hands should never hold,

This mutual kiss drop down between us both
As an unowned thing, once the lips being cold.
And Love, be false ! if *he*, to keep one oath,
Must lose one joy, by his life's star foretold.

XXXVII

Pardon, oh, pardon, that my soul should make,
Of all that strong divineness which I know
For thine and thee, an image only so
Formed of the sand, and fit to shift and break.
It is that distant years which did not take
Thy sovranty, recoiling with a blow,
Have forced my swimming brain to undergo
Their doubt and dread, and blindly to forsake
Thy purity of likeness and distort
Thy worthiest love to a worthless counterfeit:
As if a shipwrecked Pagan, safe in port,
His guardian sea-god to commemorate,
Should set a sculptured porpoise, gills a-snort
And vibrant tail, within the temple-gate.

XXXVIII

First time he kissed me, he but only kissed
The fingers of this hand wherewith I write;
And ever since, it grew more clean and white,
Slow to world-greetings, quick with its ' Oh, list,'
When the angels speak. A ring of amethyst
I could not wear here, plainer to my sight,
Than that first kiss. The second passed in height
The first, and sought the forehead, and half missed,
Half falling on the hair. O beyond meed !
That was the chrism of love, which love's own crown,
With sanctifying sweetness, did precede.
The third upon my lips was folded down
In perfect, purple state; since when, indeed,
I have been proud and said, ' My love, my own.'

XXXIX

Because thou hast the power and own'st the grace
To look through and behind this mask of me
(Against which years have beat thus blanchingly
With their rains), and behold my soul's true face,
The dim and weary witness of life's race,—
Because thou hast the faith and love to see,
Through that same soul's distracting lethargy,
The patient angel waiting for a place
In the new Heavens,—because nor sin nor woe,
Nor God's infliction, nor death's neighborhood,
Nor all which others viewing, turn to go,
Nor all which makes me tired of all, self-viewed,—
Nothing repels thee, . . . Dearest, teach me so
To pour out gratitude, as thou dost, good !

XL

Oh, yes ! they love through all this world of ours !
I will not gainsay love, called love forsooth.
I have heard love talked in my early youth,
And since, not so long back but that the flowers
Then gathered, smell still. Mussulmans and Giaours
Throw kerchiefs at a smile, and have no ruth
For any weeping. Polypheme's white tooth
Slips on the nut if, after frequent showers,
The shell is over-smooth,—and not so much
Will turn the thing called love, aside to hate
Or else to oblivion. But thou art not such
A lover, my Belovèd ! thou canst wait
Through sorrow and sickness, to bring souls to touch,
And think it soon when others cry ' Too late.'

XLI

I thank all who have loved me in their hearts,
With thanks and love from mine. Deep thanks to all
Who paused a little near the prison-wall
To hear my music in its louder parts
Ere they went onward, each one to the mart's

Or temple's occupation, beyond call.
But thou, who, in my voice's sink and fall
When the sob took it, thy divinest Art's
Own instrument didst drop down at thy foot
To hearken what I said between my tears, . . .
Instruct me how to thank thee ! Oh, to shoot
My soul's full meaning into future years,
That *they* should lend it utterance, and salute
Love that endures, from Life that disappears !

XLII

' *My future will not copy fair my past*' —
I wrote that once; and thinking at my side
My ministering life-angel justified
The word by his appealing look upcast
To the white throne of God, I turned at last,
And there, instead, saw thee, not unallied
To angels in thy soul ! Then I, long tried
By natural ills, received the comfort fast,
While budding, at thy sight, my pilgrim's staff
Gave out green leaves with morning dews impearled.
I seek no copy now of life's first half:
Leave here the pages with long musing curled,
And write me new my future's epigraph,
New angel mine, unhoped for in the world !

XLIII

How do I love thee ? Let me count the ways.
I love thee to the depth and breadth and height
My soul can reach, when feeling out of sight
For the ends of Being and ideal Grace.
I love thee to the level of everyday's
Most quiet need, by sun and candle-light.
I love thee freely, as men strive for Right;
I love thee purely, as they turn from Praise.
I love thee with the passion put to use
In my old griefs, and with my childhood's faith.
I love thee with a love I seemed to lose

With my lost saints,—I love thee with the breath,
Smiles, tears, of all my life !—and, if God choose,
I shall but love thee better after death.

XLIV

Belovèd, thou hast brought me many flowers
Plucked in the garden, all the summer through
And winter, and it seemed as if they grew
In this close room, nor missed the sun and showers.
So, in the like name of that love of ours,
Take back these thoughts which here unfolded too,
And which on warm and cold days I withdrew
From my heart's ground. Indeed, those beds and bowers
Be overgrown with bitter weeds and rue,
And wait thy weeding; yet here 's eglantine,
Here 's ivy !—take them, as I used to do
Thy flowers, and keep them where they shall not pine.
Instruct thine eyes to keep their colors true,
And tell thy soul their roots are left in mine.

A Curse for a Nation

PROLOGUE

I heard an angel speak last night,
    And he said ' Write !
Write a Nation's curse for me,
And send it over the Western Sea.'

I faltered, taking up the word:
    ' Not so, my lord !
If curses must be, choose another
To send thy curse against my brother.

' For I am bound by gratitude,
    By love and blood,
To brothers of mine across the sea,
Who stretch out kindly hands to me.'

' Therefore,' the voice said, ' shalt thou write
  My curse to-night.
From the summits of love a curse is driven,
As lightning is from the tops of heaven.'

' Not so,' I answered. ' Evermore
  My heart is sore
For my own land's sins: for little feet
Of children bleeding along the street:

' For parked-up honors that gainsay
  The right of way:
For almsgiving through a door that is
Not open enough for two friends to kiss:

' For love of freedom which abates
  Beyond the Straits:
For patriot virtue starved to vice on
Self-praise, self-interest, and suspicion:

' For an oligarchic parliament,
  And bribes well-meant.
What curse to another land assign,
When heavy-souled for the sins of mine ? '

' Therefore,' the voice said, ' shalt thou write
  My curse to-night.
Because thou hast strength to see and hate
A foul thing done *within* thy gate.'

' Not so,' I answered once again.
  ' To curse, choose men.
For I, a woman, have only known
How the heart melts and the tears run down.'

' Therefore,' the voice said, ' shalt thou write
  My curse to-night.
Some women weep and curse, I say
(And no one marvels), night and day.

' And thou shalt take their part to-night,
      Weep and write.
A curse from the depths of womanhood
Is very salt, and bitter, and good.'

So thus I wrote, and mourned indeed,
      What all may read.
And thus, as was enjoined on me,
I send it over the Western Sea.

THE CURSE

I

Because ye have broken your own chain
      With the strain
Of brave men climbing a Nation's height,
Yet thence bear down with brand and thong
On souls of others,—for this wrong
      This is the curse.   Write.

Because yourselves are standing straight
      In the state
Of Freedom's foremost acolyte,
Yet keep calm footing all the time
On writhing bond-slaves,—for this crime
      This is the curse.   Write.

Because ye prosper in God's name,
      With a claim
To honor in the old world's sight,
Yet do the fiend's work perfectly
In strangling martyrs,—for this lie
      This is the curse.   Write.

II

Ye shall watch while kings conspire
Round the people's smouldering fire,

  And, warm for your part,
Shall never dare—O shame !
To utter the thought into flame
  Which burns at your heart.
     This is the curse. Write.

Ye shall watch while nations strive
With the bloodhounds, die or survive,
  Drop faint from their jaws,
Or throttle them backward to death;
And only under your breath
  Shall favor the cause.
     This is the curse. Write.

Ye shall watch while strong men draw
The nets of feudal law
  To strangle the weak;
And, counting the sin for a sin,
Your soul shall be sadder within
  Than the word ye shall speak.
     This is the curse. Write.

When good men are praying erect
That Christ may avenge his elect
  And deliver the earth,
The prayer in your ears, said low,
Shall sound like the tramp of a foe
  That 's driving you forth.
     This is the curse. Write.

When wise men give you their praise,
They shall pause in the heat of the phrase,
  As if carried too far.
When ye boast your own charters kept true,
Ye shall blush; for the thing which ye do
  Derides what ye are.
     This is the curse. Write.

When fools cast taunts at your gate,
Your scorn ye shall somewhat abate
   As ye look o'er the wall;
For your conscience, tradition, and name
Explode with a deadlier blame
   Than the worst of them all.
         This is the curse.   Write.

Go, wherever ill deeds shall be done,
Go, plant your flag in the sun
   Beside the ill-doers !
And recoil from clenching the curse
Of God's witnessing Universe
   With a curse of yours.
         This is the curse.   Write.

A False Step

Sweet, thou hast trod on a heart.
   Pass; there 's a world full of men;
And women as fair as thou art
   Must do such things now and then.

Thou hast only stepped unaware,—
   Malice, not one can impute;
And why should a heart have been there
   In the way of a fair woman's foot ?

It was not a stone that could trip,
   Nor was it a thorn that could rend:
Put up thy proud under-lip !
   'T was merely the heart of a friend.

And yet peradventure one day
   Thou, sitting alone at the glass,

Remarking the bloom gone away,
   Where the smile in its dimplement was,

And seeking around thee in vain
   From hundreds who flattered before,
Such a word as ' Oh, not in the main
   Do I hold thee less precious, but more ! ' . . .

Thou 'lt sigh, very like, on thy part,
   ' Of all I have known or can know,
I wish I had only that Heart
   I trod upon ages ago ! '

Amy's Cruelty

Fair Amy of the terraced house,
   Assist me to discover
Why you who would not hurt a mouse
   Can torture so your lover.

You give your coffee to the cat,
   You stroke the dog for coming,
And all your face grows kinder at
   The little brown bee's humming.

But when *he* haunts your door . . . the town
   Marks coming and marks going . . .
You seem to have stitched your eyelids down
   To that long piece of sewing !

You never give a look, not you,
   Nor drop him a ' Good morning,'
To keep his long day warm and blue,
   So fretted by your scorning.

She shook her head—' The mouse and bee
   For crumb or flower will linger:

The dog is happy at my knee,
    The cat purrs at my finger.

' But *he* . . . to *him*, the least thing given
    Means great things at a distance;
He wants my world, my sun, my heaven,
    Soul, body, whole existence.

' They say love gives as well as takes;
    But I 'm a simple maiden,—
My mother's first smile when she wakes
    I still have smiled and prayed in.

' I only know my mother's love
    Which gives all and asks nothing;
And this new loving sets the groove
    Too much the way of loathing.

' Unless he gives me all in change,
    I forfeit all things by him:
The risk is terrible and strange—
    I tremble, doubt, . . . deny him.

' He 's sweetest friend or hardest foe,
    Best angel or worst devil;
I either hate or . . . love him so,
    I can't be merely civil !

' You trust a woman who puts forth
    Her blossoms thick as summer's ?
You think she dreams what love is worth,
    Who casts it to new-comers ?

' Such love 's a cowslip-ball to fling,
    A moment's pretty pastime;
I give . . . all me, if anything,
    The first time and the last time.

' Dear neighbor of the trellised house,
    A man should murmur never,
Though treated worse than dog and mouse,
    Till doated on for ever ! '

A Musical Instrument

I

What was he doing, the great god Pan,
    Down in the reeds by the river ?
Spreading ruin and scattering ban,
Splashing and paddling with hoofs of a goat,
And breaking the golden lilies afloat
    With the dragon-fly on the river.

II

He tore out a reed, the great god Pan,
    From the deep cool bed of the river:
The limpid water turbidly ran,
And the broken lilies a-dying lay,
And the dragon-fly had fled away,
    Ere he brought it out of the river.

III

High on the shore sat the great god Pan
    While turbidly flowed the river;
And hacked and hewed as a great god can,
With his hard bleak steel at the patient reed,
Till there was not a sign of the leaf indeed
    To prove it fresh from the river.

IV

He cut it short, did the great god Pan,
    (How tall it stood in the river !)
Then drew the pith, like the heart of a man,
Steadily from the outside ring,
And notched the poor dry empty thing
    In holes, as he sat by the river.

V

' This is the way,' laughed the great god Pan
    (Laughed while he sat by the river),
' The only way, since gods began
To make sweet music, they could succeed.'

Then, dropping his mouth to a hole in the reed,
    He blew in power by the river.

VI

Sweet, sweet, sweet, O Pan !
    Piercing sweet by the river !
Blinding sweet, O great god Pan !
The sun on the hill forgot to die,
And the lilies revived, and the dragon-fly
    Came back to dream on the river.

VII

Yet half a beast is the great god Pan,
    To laugh as he sits by the river,
Making a poet out of a man:
The true gods sigh for the cost and pain,—
For the reed which grows nevermore again
    As a reed with the reeds in the river.

The Forced Recruit

SOLFERINO, 1859

In the ranks of the Austrian you found him,
    He died with his face to you all;
Yet bury him here where around him
    You honor your bravest that fall.

Venetian, fair-featured and slender,
    He lies shot to death in his youth,
With a smile on his lips over-tender
    For any mere soldier's dead mouth.

No stranger, and yet not a traitor,
    Though alien the cloth on his breast,
Underneath it how seldom a greater
    Young heart has a shot sent to rest !

By your enemy tortured and goaded
　　To march with them, stand in their file,
His musket (see) never was loaded,
　　He facing your guns with that smile !

As orphans yearn on to their mothers,
　　He yearned to your patriot bands;—
' Let me die for our Italy, brothers,
　　If not in your ranks, by your hands !

' Aim straightly, fire steadily ! spare me
　　A ball in the body which may
Deliver my heart here, and tear me
　　This badge of the Austrian away ! '

So thought he, so died he this morning.
　　What then ? many others have died.
Ay, but easy for men to die scorning
　　The death-stroke, who fought side by side—

One tricolor floating above them;
　　Struck down 'mid triumphant acclaims
Of an Italy rescued to love them
　　And blazon the brass with their names.

But he,—without witness or honor,
　　Mixed, shamed in his country's regard,
With the tyrants who march in upon her,
　　Died faithful and passive: 't was hard.

'T was sublime. In a cruel restriction
　　Cut off from the guerdon of sons,
With most filial obedience, conviction,
　　His soul kissed the lips of her guns.

That moves you ? Nay, grudge not to show it,
　　While digging a grave for him here:
The others who died, says your poet,
　　Have glory,—let *him* have a tear.

Alphabetical List of Titles

	page
Amy's Cruelty	47
Cheerfulness Taught by Reason	5
Consolation	4
Cry of the Children, The	7
Cry of the Human, The	16
Curse for a Nation, A	42
False Step, A	46
Forced Recruit, The	50
Grief	4
Hiram Powers' 'Greek Slave'	21
Life and Love	23
Musical Instrument, A	49
Sea-Side Walk, A	3
Sleep, The	1
Sonnets from the Portuguese	24
To Flush, My Dog	12
To George Sand: A Desire	6
To George Sand: A Recognition	6
Two Sketches	20
Woman's Shortcomings, A	21

Alphabetical List of First Lines

Each sonnet in *Sonnets from the Portuguese*, each of the "Two Sketches" and each part of "A Curse for a Nation" is listed separately.

	page
Accuse me not, beseech thee, that I wear	30
A heavy heart, Belovèd, have I borne	34
All are not taken; there are left behind	4
And therefore if to love can be desert	28
And wilt thou have me fashion into speech	29
And yet, because thou overcomest so	30
Because thou hast the power and own'st the grace —	40
Because ye have broken your own chain	44
Belovèd, my Belovèd, when I think	32
Belovèd, thou hast brought me many flowers	42
But only three in all God's universe	24
Can it be right to give what I can give?	27
Do ye hear the children weeping, O my brothers	7
Fair Amy of the terraced house	47
Fast this Life of mine was dying	23
First time he kissed me, he but only kissed	39
Go from me. Yet I feel that I shall stand	26
Her azure eyes, dark lashes hold in fee	20
How do I love thee? Let me count the ways	41
If I leave all for thee, wilt thou exchange	38
If thou must love me, let it be for nought	29
I heard an angel speak last night	42
I lift my heavy heart up solemnly	25
I lived with visions for my company	34
Indeed this very love which is my boast	28

I never gave a lock of hair away	31
In the ranks of the Austrian you found him	50
I see thine image through my tears to-night	36
Is it indeed so? If I lay here dead	33
I tell you, hopeless grief is passionless	4
I thank all who have loved me in their hearts	40
I think of thee!—my thoughts do twine and bud	35
I think we are too ready with complaint	5
I thought once how Theocritus had sung	24
Let the world's sharpness, like a clasping knife	33
Loving friend, the gift of one	12
'My future will not copy fair my past'—	41
My letters! all dead paper, mute and white!	35
My poet, thou canst touch on all the notes	30
My own Belovèd, who hast lifted me	35
Of all the thoughts of God that are	1
Oh, yes! they love through all this world of ours!	40
Pardon, oh, pardon, that my soul should make	39
Say over again, and yet once over again	32
She has laughed as softly as if she sighed	21
Sweet, thou hast trod on a heart	46
The face of all the world is changed, I think	26
The first time that the sun rose on thine oath	37
'There is no God' the foolish saith	16
The shadow of her face upon the wall	20
The soul's Rialto hath its merchandise	31
They say Ideal beauty cannot enter	21
Thou comest! all is said without a word	36
Thou hast thy calling to some palace-floor	25
Thou large-brained woman and large-hearted man	6
True genius, but true woman! dost deny	6
Unlike are we, unlike, O princely Heart!	24
We walked beside the sea	3
What can I give thee back, O liberal	27
What was he doing, the great god Pan	49
When our two souls stand up erect and strong	32
When we met first and loved, I did not build	38
With the same heart, I said, I'll answer thee	37
Yes, call me by my pet-name! let me hear	37
Yet love, mere love, is beautiful indeed	27